Silly Mammo

An Ethiopian Tale

Kilu Mammo
ቂሉ ማሞ

Retold by Gebregeorgis Yohannes

Illustrated by Bogale Belachew

AFRICAN SUN PUBLISHING
for Ethiopian Books for Children
& Educational Foundation

To my children Kaleb & Alula and all the children of Ethiopia –GY

English text copyright ©2002 by Gebregeorgis Yohannes
Amharic text copyright ©2002 by Gebregeorgis Yohannes
Illustrations copyright ©2002 by Ethiopian Books for Children & Educational Foundation (EBCEF)

Title: Silly Mammo, An Ethiopian Tale
English – Amharic

ISBN 1-883701-04-x

Price: $10.00 U.S.

Acknowledgments:

The publishing of this book was possible by the generous financial support
of the Presbyterian Church of Grand Forks North Dakota and the Presbytery of
the Northern Plains, with donations from several other friends of Ethiopia.

EBCEF would like to thank Janie Bynum (www.janiebynum.com) for donating
the design and production of this book and arranging the printing.
We would also like to thank children's author Jane Kurtz (www.janekurtz.com)
for fundraising and coordinating the publishing of this book.

This book published by African Sun Publishing for Ethiopian Books for
Children & Educational Foundation (EBCEF).

Printed in the United States by Dickinson Press, Grand Rapids Michigan.

Before you begin:

In Ethiopian storytelling tradition, it's customary for children to sit wide-eyed, in front of the storyteller.

The storyteller starts by saying, "Teret! Teret!"
(which means: "A story! A story!")

The children reply, "Ye lam beret!" (This literally means: "a cow's pen," but when used in this way means that they want told to them as many stories as could fill a cow's pen.)

Or sometimes children reply, "Yemeseret" (This literally means: "of the foundation;" meaning stories that are deep in the culture or tradition.)

Only then does the storyteller start telling, and telling and telling, late into the starry night until the children are sleepy.

Glossary in back of book.

"Teret! teret!"
"Ye lam beret!"

ተረት! ተረት!
የላም በረት!

A long time ago, in Ethiopia, there lived a boy called Mammo. Mammo and his mother *Weizero* Terunesh lived in a small *tukul* on the outskirts of a town.

በድሮ ጊዜ በኢትዮጵያ ሀገር የሚኖር ማሞ የሚባል ወጣት ነበር። ማሞና እናቱ ወይዘሮ ጥሩነሽ የሚኖሩት ከአንድ ከተማ ትንሽ ወጣ ብለው በአንድ ደሳሳ ጎጆ ነበር።

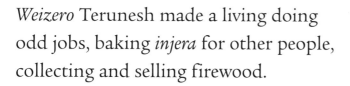

Weizero Terunesh made a living doing odd jobs, baking *injera* for other people, collecting and selling firewood.

Mammo, however, did not work because his mother was afraid he could not hold down a job.

ወይዘሮ ጥሩነሽ የሚተዳደሩት በሰው ቤት እንጀራ በመጋገር፤ እንጨት እየለቀሙ በመሸጥና ሌላም ያገኙትን ሥራ ሁሉ በመሥራት ነበር።

ማሞ ግን ምንም ሥራ አይሠራም፤ እናቱ ሥራ መቆየት አይችልም ብለው ይፈሩ ነበር።

At the same time Mammo had a very big appetite. He ate three pieces of *injera* mixed with sauce for breakfast and six *injeras* with meat sauce and *ayb* for lunch and dinner. Mammo was very strong and handsome. His mother was always happy seeing Mammo eat. But sometimes she worried about what would happen to her son, because Mammo was very silly.

ከዝያም በላይ ማሞ የምግብ ፍላጎቱ በጣም ብዙ ነበር። ለቁርስ የሶስት እንጀራ ፍትፍት፣ ለምሳና ለራት ደግሞ ስድስት ስድስት እንጀራ በሥጋ ወጥ፣ ከቅልጥም፣ ከአይብና እርጎ ጋር ነበር የሚበላው። ማሞ በጣም ጠንካራና ቁመናው ያማረ ጉብል ነበር። እናቱ ትልቁ ደስታቸው ማሞ ሲበላ ማየት ነበር። በልቶ የሚጠግብ አይመስላቸውም። ግን በብርቱ የሚያሳስባቸው ጉዳይ ቢኖር የማሞ ቂልነት ነበር።

Whenever children saw Mammo on the street, they would follow him and shout, "Kilu Mammo! Kilu Mammo!" They would stick out their tongues at him, climb on him and sometimes wrestle him. Mammo only laughed and never was angry with the children.

"They get tired soon enough," he would say, "And then they leave me alone."

የአካባቢው ልጆች ማሞን ባዩት ቁጥር 'ቂሉ ማሞ ! ቂሉ ማሞ ! ' እያሉ ይከታተሉታል፤ አፍንጫቸው ድረስ ቀርበው ምላሳቸውን ያወጡብታል፤ ይንጠላጠሉብታል፤ ትግል ይገጥሙታል። ማሞ ግን ከመሳቅ በስተቀር አይቆጣቸውም። 'ሲደክማቸው ይተዉኛል ' ይላል።

One day *Weizero* Terunesh called Mammo and said, "Now listen carefully and obey me, my dear son, Mammo. From now on you have to look for work and help me with expenses. I am getting old and too tired to work as I used to."

አንድ ቀን ወይዘሮ ጥሩነሽ ማሞን ጠርተው 'ውድ ልጄ ማሞ በጥሞና አድምጠኝ፤ የምልህንም ፈፅም፤ ከአሁን ጀምሮ ሥራ እየፈለክ መስራት አለብህ። እኔ እንደቀድሞዬ ለመሥራት አቅሜ እየደከመ ነው' አሉት።

"*Eshi emama*, I'll help you. But how do I find work?" Mammo asked, looking at his mother lovingly.

'እሺ እማማ! የምችለውን ሁሉ እሠራለሁ ለመሆኑ ሥራ እንዴት ነው የሚገኘው?' አለ ማሞ እናቱን ፍቅር በተሞላበት ዐይታ እየተመለከተ።

"Go to that rich farmer," said his mother. "People around here always need strong young men."

'ከዝያ ሀብታም ገበሬ ጋ ሂድ፤ ሁልጊዜም ጠንካራ፤ ወጣት ጉልበት ይፈልጋሉ' አሉ እናቱ።

The next day, Mammo found work at the farm. After working all day he was paid two *semunis*. Mammo was walking home when he stumbled and fell, and the two *semunis* slipped out of his grip and disappeared. Since Mammo had never had money before, he did not know to put the *semunis* in his pocket.

When he got home his mother listened to his story and then scolded him. "Be sure to obey me," she said. "Next time remember to put it in your pocket."

"*Eshi emama*, I'll do as you said next time," said Mammo.

በሚቀጥለው ቀን ማሞ ከገበሬው ዘንድ ሥራ አገኘ። ቀኑን በሙሉ ሲሠራ ውሎ ሁለት ስመኒ ተከፈለው። ማሞ ወደቤቱ ሲሄድ አደናቅፍት ወደቀ። በእጁ ጨቡዶ የያዛቸው ሁለት ስመኒዎች ከእጁ ተስፈትልከው ጠፉ። ማሞ ካሁን ቀደም ገንዘብ ኖሮት ስለማያውቅ ስመኒዎቹን ኪሱ ውስጥ መጨመር አንዳለበት አላወቀም።

እቤት ሲደርስ እናቱ የሆነውን ከሰሙ በሀዋላ ተቆጡት።

'የምልህን አድምጥ፣ በሚቀጥለው ጊዜ ኪስህ ውስጥ መጨመር አትርሳ' አለት።

እሺ እማማ! በሚቀጥለው ጊዜ እንዳልሽኝ አደርጋለሁ' አለ ማሞ።

The next day Mammo got work with a cattle herder. After his day's work he was given a bottle of milk. Mammo remembered his mother's advice from the first day. Carefully, he poured all the milk from the bottle in his pocket. When he got home the bottle was empty.

"Oh, Mammo," his mother said. "Next time you must remember to carry your wages on your head."

"*Eshi emama*," Mammo said, "I'll do as you said next time."

በሚቀጥለው ቀን ማሞ ከአንድ ከብት አርቢ ዘንድ ሲሠራ ዋለ። ለሥራው ክፍያ አንድ ጠርሙስ ወተት ተሰጠው። ባለፈው ቀን እናቱ ያሉት ትዝ አለው። ጠርሙሱን ወተት ከኪሱ ዶለው። ቤቱ ሲደርስ ወተቱ ሁሉ ፈስሶ ባዶ ጠርሙስ ብቻ ነበር የቀረው።

እናቱም ማሞን ተቆጡት። 'በሚቀጥለው ጊዜ በራስህ ላይ አድርገው' አሉት።

'እሺ እማማ! በሚቀጥለው ጊዜ እንዳልሽኝ አደር ጋለሁ' አለ ማሞ።

The next day Mammo worked again with the cattle herder. At the end of the day the herder gave him some butter wrapped in banana leaves to take home. Mammo remembered his mother's advice. Proudly, he put the butter on his head and headed home. But it was a warm and sunny day and all the butter melted on Mammo's head.

When he got home his mother couldn't help but smile. Then she said, "Next time remember to hold it firmly with your hands."

Mammo rubbed his buttery head and said, "*Eshi emama*, I'll do as you said next time."

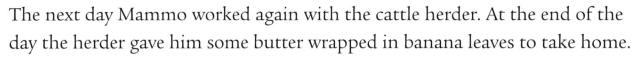

በሚቀጥለው ቀን ማሞ ዳግመኛ ከከብት አርቢው ዘንድ ሲሠራ ዋለ። ለሥራውም ክፍያ በኮባ የተጠቀለለ ቅቤ ተሰጠው። ባለፈው ቀን እናቱ ያሉት ትዝ አለው። በኩራት ቅቤውን እንደተጠቀለለ እራሱ ላይ አደረገው። ቀኑ ሞቃታማ ስለነበር ቀስ በቀስ ቅቤው እራሱ ላይ ቀለጠ አለቀ። ማሞ እቤቱ ሲደርስ እናቱ ሲያዩት ሳቃቸው መጣ። ከዝያም 'በሚቀጥለው ጊዜ በእጅህ እቅፍ አድርገህ መያዝ አትርሳ' አሉት።

'እሺ እማማ! በሚቀጥለው ጊዜ እንዳልሸኝ አደርጋለሁ' አለ ማሞ በቅቤ የራሰ ራሱን እያሻሸ።

The next day, Mammo got work with a grain merchant. After a day's work the merchant picked one of the skinniest of his many cats and gave it to Mammo.

"Here, this cat will catch you lots of rats," said the merchant proudly.

Mammo took the cat and remembered his mother's advice. He held the cat tightly with his two hands and started home.

Soon, the cat started screeching and scratching at Mammo. Mammo dropped the cat and it dashed off.

When Mammo told his mother what had happened, she sighed. "Next time remember to tie it with a rope and pull it."

"*Eshi emama*, I'll do as you said next time," said Mammo.

በሴላ ቀን ማሞ ከአንድ የእሕል ነጋዴ ዘንድ ሲሠራ ዋለ። ነጋዴውም የእሕል ነተራውን ከሚጠብቁለት ብዙ ድመቶች መሃል አንዲት ከሲታዋን መርጦ ለማሞ ሰጠው። 'እንካ፤ ይሕች ድመት ብዙ አይጥ ትይዝልሃለች' አለ ነጋዴው በኩራት። ማሞም ድመትዋን ተቀበለ። ባለፈው ቀን እናቱ ያሉት ትዝ አለው። ድመቲቱን በቅጠል ጠቅልሎ በሁለት እጆቹ እቅፍ አድርጎ መንገዱን ቀጠለ። ጥቂት እንደሄደ ድመቲቱ ማሞን ሞኘጭጭራና ነክሳ ከእጁ ተስፈትልካ አመለጠችው።

እቤቱ ሲደርስ ማሞ የሆነውን ለእናቱ ነገራቸው። እሳቸውም በጣም አዘኑ። በሚቀጥለው ጊዜ በገመድ ጥፍር አድርገህ አስረህ መንተት አትርሳ አሉት።

'እሺ እማማ! በሚቀጥለው ጊዜ እንዳልሽኝ አደርጋለሁ' አለ ማሞ።

The next day, Mammo found work at a butcher's. By midday he was given a big ox leg to take home for his mother to cook for dinner. Remembering his mother's scolding the day before, Mammo tied the ox leg with a rope and started on his way pulling it behind him.

በሚቀጥለው ቀን ማሞ ከአንድ የልኩዋንዳ ቤት ሲሥራ ዋለ። እኩለ ቀን ላይ ልኩዋንዳ አራጁ ለማሞ አንድ የበሬ ታፋ ሰጡት። ማሞ ባለፈው ቀን እናቱ ያሉት ትዝ አለው። ስጋውን በገመድ ጠፍር አሰረ። እየጎተተም ወደ ቤቱ ጉዞ ቀጠለ።

Soon, all the hungry neighborhood dogs smelled the meat and followed Mammo, stealing chunks from the meat. Children saw Mammo and followed him laughing.

Old men and old women on the sidewalk saw Mammo and the dogs and the children and pointed their fingers and laughed heartily. Mammo calmly minded his own business.

ስጋውን ያሸተቱ የተራቡ የመንደር ውሾች ማሞን እየተከታተሉ ስጋወን መነተፉበት። ይህንን ያዩ የመንደር ልጆች ሁሉ ማሞን እየተከታተሉ ሳቁበት። በየመንገዱ ዳር ያሉ አዛውንቶችና ባልቴቶችም ሁሉ ጣታቸውን ወደ ማሞ እየቀሰሩ ተሳሳቁ። ማሞ በእርጋታ መንገዱን ቀጠለ።

When Mammo arrived home, only the bone was left.

"Well!" his mother said, "I hope next time you will remember to carry it on your back."

"*Eshi emama*, I'll do as you said next time," he said.

ማሞ ቤቱ ሲደርስ ውሾቹ ስጋውን በሙሉ ሙልጭ አርገው የተረው አጥንቱ ብቻ ነበር። እናቱ በማዘን 'እንግዲህ በሚቀጥለው ጊዜ አስታውሰህ በትክሻህ ላይ እንደምትሸከም ተስፋ አደርጋለሁ' አለት።

'እሺ እማማ! በሚቀጥለው ጊዜ እንዳልሽኝ አደርጋለሁ' አለ ማሞ።

In a small town near Mammo's village, there lived a young maiden named Tewabech. She was beautiful, but she could neither hear nor speak.

ማሞ ከሚኖርበት መንደር አቅራብያ በአንድ ትንሽ ከተማ የምትኖር፣ የማትነገርና የማትሰማ ተዋበች የምትባል ውብ ቆንጆ ኮረዳ ነበረች።

Tewabech's father, *Negadras* Tessema was a wealthy small town merchant. He had tirelessly searched for a cure for Tewabech. He had visited many *hakims* and *awakis* far and wide, but to no avail. Once, however, a *menoksit* had whispered to him that Tewabech could be cured only if she could laugh.

የተዋበች አባት ነጋድራስ ተሰማ ባለብዙ ሃብት ነጋዴ ቢሆኑም ለአንድ ልጃቸው ፈውስ አልገኙላትም። ያልደረሱበት ሐኪም፣ ያልደረሱበት አዋቂ አልነበረም ግን ምንም መፍትሄ አላገኙም። አንዲት የዘጉ መነኩሲት ግን 'ተዋበች መዳን የምትችለው አንድ ጊዜ ከሳቀች ብቻ ነው' ብለው ነበር።

That very day, *Negadras* Tessema made an *awaj* by the town crier.

"Awaj! Awaj! Awaj!
You, who have not heard, listen!
You, who have heard, tell others!
Negadras Tessema, hereby proclaims,
He who shall make my daughter laugh,
Be he a wise man or a lad,
He shall have her for a wife!"

But no one could make Tewabech laugh.

ያንኑ ቀን ነጋድራስ ተሰማ በከተማው አዋጅ አስነገሩ።

'አዋጅ! አዋጅ! አዋጅ!
የደበሉ ቅዳጅ!
ያልሰማህ ስማ!
የሰማህ ላልሰማ አሰማ!
እኔ ነጋድራስ ተሰማ!
ልጄን ያሳቀ ሊቅ ይሁን ደቂቅ፤
እጅዋን እሰጠዋለሁ፣ እሽልመዋለሁ!'

ነገር ግን ተዋቦችን ምንም የሚያስቃት አልተገኘም።

Most days Tewabech would sit
by the window of the second floor
of her house looking down on
the passersby.

ተዋበች አብዛኛውን ቀን በትልቁ
ቤታቸው ሁለተኛ ደርብ በመስኮት
አጠገብ ተቀምጣ አላፊና አግዳሚውን
ስታይ ነው የምትውለው።

Mammo, meanwhile, had found work with a cattle merchant. After a week's work, the merchant gave Mammo a *wurinchila* donkey. Mammo remembered his mother's advice, so he picked up the little donkey and put it on his shoulders and started home.

ከብዙ ጊዜ በህዋላ ማሞ አንድ ቀን ከአንድ ከብት ነጋዴ ዘንድ ለአንድ ሳምንት ሲሠራ ሰነበተ። ነጋዴውም ለማሞ አንድ የአህያ ውርንጭላ ሰጠው። ማሞም ባለፈው ቀን እናቱ ያሉት ትዝ አለው። ትንሸዋን ውርንጭላ አንከብክቦ ትከሻው ላይ አድርጎ ጉዞ ቀጠለ።

As Mammo passed by the house of *Negadras* Tessema, Tewabech was perched by the window as usual, gazing sadly into the street. Down the street came Mammo, stumbling unsteadily. On his back, the uncomfortable donkey brayed and kicked its four legs.

Tewabech stared at Mammo and the donkey. All of a sudden Tewabech burst out laughing.

Ha! Ha! Ha! Ha! Ha! Ha!

Ha! Ha! Ha! Ha! Ha! Ha!

It was almost a donkey laugh.

በአጋጣሚ ማሞ የሚያልፈው በነጋድራስ
ተሰማ ቤት በኩል ነበር፡፡ ተዋበችም
እንደልማድዋ በመስኮቱ አጠገብ ቁጭ
ብላ ብዝዙን መንገድ መንገዱን ታይ ነበር፡፡
ማሞም አህያዋን እንደተሸከመ እየተንገዳገደ
ሲጌድ አህያዋም ስላልተመቻት እግሮችዋን
ታወራጭ ነበር፡፡ በዚህን ጊዜ ተዋበች ማሞንና
አህያዋን ተመለከተች፡፡ በነገሩም በታም ተደነቀች
በድንገት ከት ብላ ሳቀች፤

ሀ! ሀ! ሀ! ሀ! ሀ! ሀ!
ሀ! ሀ! ሀ! ሀ! ሀ! ሀ!

የአህያ አይነት ሳቅ ነበር፡፡

Negadras Tessema, who was next door, was startled by this unusual and strange laughter. He bolted out and rushed to Tewabech's room.

"*Ababa! Ababa!* look at that funny person and the *wurinchila* donkey he is carrying!" Tewabech said, pointing to Mammo.

ነጋድራስ ተሰማ በሚቀጥለው ክፍል ውስጥ ነበሩ። ሰምተው የማያውቁት ሳቅ ሲሰሙ ተደናግጠው ተዋበች ወዳለችበት ክፍል ሮጠው ገቡ።

'አባባ! አባባ! ተመልከት ያንን የሚያስቅ ሰውና ወርንጭላውን' አለች ጣትዋን ወደ ማሞ ቀስራ።

Negadras Tessema was full of joy. He ran downstairs, grabbed Mammo by the hand and led him into the house. Mammo was confused, but he was an obedient fellow, so he didn't complain.

"You have cured my daughter! You shall marry her! From today on you are my son," proclaimed *Negadras* Tessema.

ነጋድራስ ተዋበች ስትንነገር በመስማታቸው በጣም ተደሰቱ። ሮጠው ወደ ማጮ ደረሱ። እጁን ይዘው እየነተቱ ወደ ቤታቸው አስገቡት። ማጮ ለጊዜው ግር ቢለውም ታዛዥ በመሆኑ ይዘዉ ሲሄዱ አልተቃወመም።

ልጄን ስላዳንካት እጅዋን ሰጥቸሃለሁ፤ ከዛሬ ጀምሮ ልጄ ነህ' አሉ ነጋድራስ ተሰማ።

Mammo looked at Tewabech and fell in love with her.

Tewabech looked at Mammo and fell in love with him.

ማሞ ተዋብችን ተመለከታት፤ ወድያውኑ ወደዳት።
ተዋበች ማሞን ተመለከተችው፤ ወድያውኑ ወደድችው።

A few days later, Mammo and Tewabech were married. *Negadras* Tessema gave the biggest wedding feast ever witnessed in the small town.

Mammo and Tewabech lived happily for many years. *Weizero* Terunesh was very happy that her son was obedient and that her daughter in law was observant and wise.

ከጥቂት ቀኖች በኋላ ማሞና ተዋበች ተጋቡ። ነጋድራስ ተሰማ በዝያች ትንሽ ከተማ ታይቶ የማይታወቅ ሰርግ ደገሱ። ማሞና ተዋበች ለብዙ ዘመን በደስታ ኖሩ። ወይዘሮ ጥሩነሽም በልጃቸው ታዛዥነትና በተዋበች አስተዋይነትና ብልህነት በጣም ተደሰቱ።

Glossary

Ababa – daddy [*Abat* means father]

Awaj – a traditional proclamation by a crier beating a drum with a message from a king or a noble usually at a market place

Awaki(s) – a wise person who is consulted for advice for all sorts of problems. A traditional healer

Ayb – homemade cheese

Emama – mom

Ergo – homemade yogurt

Eshi – okay or yes

Hakim – a physician or doctor; medical professional

Injera – flat, thin Ethiopian staple bread

Kil / Kilu – silly / the silly

Menekusit – a female monk

Negadras – head of merchants; a traditional title

Semuni(s) – Ethiopian quarter [twenty-five *santim* (cents)]

Terunesh – a female name meaning "you are good"

Tessema – a male name meaning "he who is listened to"

Tukul – a grass hut

Tewabech – a female name meaning "she is beautiful"

Weizero – Ethiopian for "Mrs."

Wurinchila – a very young donkey